Take Time To RELAX!

By Nancy Carlson

🌿 Carolrhoda Books • Minneapolis

C-0
8-17

Carolrhoda Books
A division of Lerner Publishing Group, Inc.
241 First Avenue North
Minneapolis, MN 55401 U.S.A.

Website address: www.lernerbooks.com

Library of Congress Cataloging-in-Publication Data Available.
ISBN: 978-0-7613-8949-1

Manufactured in the United States of America
1 – HF – 12/31/11

Dedicated to busy people everywhere. –NC

Tina and her parents were always busy.

On Mondays, Tina had ballet class.

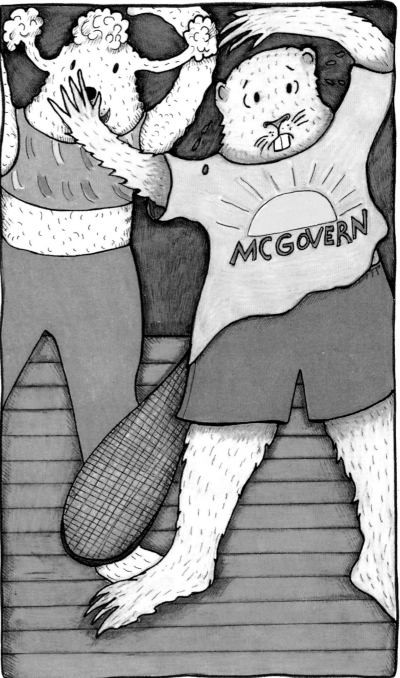

Mom worked late while Dad took aerobics.

On Tuesday nights, Dad drove Tina to volleyball.

Then he went to cake-decorating class.

On Wednesdays, Tina rushed to swimming class.

Dad took computer class and Mom took aerobics.

On Thursday nights, Dad and Tina ate dinner in the car while they rushed Tina to karate class.

On Fridays, Dad went to bridge club while Mom played tennis.

On Saturdays, they worked and worked around the house.

By the time Sundays came, Tina, Mom, and Dad were exhausted from their busy week.

Day after day, week after week, Tina and her parents
rushed around. Until one morning . . .

. . . it was snowing like crazy.

"All the roads are closed," said Dad.

"But I have computer club and dance!" said Tina.

"I have a big meeting!" said Mom.

"What will we do?"

"Let's make a big breakfast!" said Mom.

"Let's build a fire," said Dad.

"Why don't you get your guitar, Dad," said Mom.

Dad sang and played his guitar.

"I'd forgotten how well you play," said Mom.

Tina didn't even know her dad could play the guitar.

Then Mom told stories about her canoe trips.

"Wow," said Tina, "can we go on a trip like that?"

Later, they made popcorn and Tina told scary stories.

"This is fun," said Dad.

"I hope it never stops snowing," said Tina.

It was late afternoon when the snow stopped.
The plows cleared the streets.

"I guess I could get a few hours in at the office," said Mom.

"I suppose I could go to computer club," said Tina.

"I could just make it to aerobics," said Dad.

"NAHHH!"

"We're having too much fun!" said Mom and Dad.

"Get the popcorn," said Tina.

"Play another song," said Mom.